This book is dedicated to Kevin Howard and inspired by his real-life story. Thank you for allowing us the pleasure of getting to know your sweet and loving dog.

www.mascotbooks.com

Are You A Pineapple?

For more information, please contact:
Mascot Books
620 Herndon Parkway, Suite 320
Herndon, VA 20170
info@mascotbooks.com

Library of Congress Control Number: 2021921773

CPSIA Code: PRT1121A

ISBN-13: 978-1-63755-145-5

Printed in the United States

ARE YOU A Pineapple?

Kathryn A. Zolman

ILLUSTRATED BY WALTER POLICELLI

Kevin has a new puppy!

"I love you so much, puppy!" Kevin says. "You are my new best friend! What should I name you?" Kevin thinks for a moment. "Should I call you **LADY?**"

The puppy just stares at Kevin.

"I feel so lucky to have you, puppy. That's it! I should name you **Lucky!**"

The puppy yawns.

"Look, puppy! The girls are having so much fun pretending in their castle. Hmmm. . . maybe you are a **PRINCESS?**"

The puppy looks away.

"You are special to me, puppy! You need a special name! What about

PEPPER?"

The puppy plops on the floor.

"I wouldn't trade you for a bazillion dollars, puppy! Not even for this shiny, new penny. Hey, is your name **PENNY?**"

The puppy covers her eyes.

"Puppy, you are prettier than Momma's flowers. Oh, I have the perfect name! Do you want to be named **Lilly** or *Daisy?*"

The puppy falls asleep.

"Wow, naming a puppy is harder than I thought. You are a one-of-a-kind, smart puppy! I guess you will let me know when I say the right name."

Kevin tries all the names he can think of:

"Come here, **Tomato!**

Sit, **Spoon!**

Shake, **SUGAR!"**

The puppy walks away.

"TOASTER?

COFFEE?

Pineapple?"
Kevin calls to
the puppy.

"Are you a *Pineapple,* puppy? Is that your name?" The puppy jumps on Kevin and gives him tons of kisses.

"Pineapple, I am so proud of you for picking the perfect name, just for you! You make me so happy!" Pineapple walks proudly beside Kevin with a big smile on her face.

Kevin has a new best friend!
And her name is

Pineapple!

About the Author

Kathryn A. Zolman never expected to write a children's book, but when Pineapple came into her life and she heard the story of how this sweet, smart dog got her name, she thought it would make a fun book for parents to read to their children. Pineapple is a Bull Mastiff, German Shepherd, Chow mix, and much like a real pineapple, she knows how to stand tall and is very sweet on the inside!

Kathryn is an avid dog lover. Along with her husband and daughter, they have raised three Doberman Pinschers, each with their own unique personality and character. Kathryn is an advocate for not only raising children to respect all animals, but also to be thankful for the pure joy that they bring to our lives. In writing this book, Kathryn seeks to spread a positive message and hopes it will help children express more gratitude in their lives.